Walt Disney's
Mickey Mouse and His Boat

Written by Alice Hughes

Illustrated by Richard Walz

A Golden Book • New York
Western Publishing Company, Inc., Racine, Wisconsin 53404

Mickey Mouse had a boat.
It was a little boat.
It had room for Mickey
and Pluto.

Mickey fished from his boat.
He watched the birds.
He talked to Pluto.

Mickey was happy.
He had his boat.
He had his dog.
What more did he need?

One day Morty and Ferdie
wanted to go fishing.

"But there is no room,"
said Mickey.
"There is no room
for Pluto."

Pluto watched the boat.
He barked and barked.
He wanted to go, too.

Mickey started to fish.
Morty and Ferdie
started to fish, too.

Something pulled at
Mickey's line.
"A fish!" he cried.
"Pull it in!" cried Ferdie.

Mickey pulled.
Mickey pulled Ferdie
into the water.

"There is no room,"
said Mickey.
"Next time only Pluto
will go."

But the next day
Minnie Mouse
wanted to go.
So did Clarabelle Cow.

"There is no room,"
said Mickey.
"There is a lot of room,"
said Clarabelle.

She sat down.
"See?" she said.
"I see," said Mickey.

They all got out
of the water.

"You need a bigger boat,"
said Minnie.
She took Mickey to
buy a boat.

Mickey bought a
big boat.
He gave his little boat
to Goofy.

The next day
Mickey went fishing.
Minnie and Clarabelle
went, too.
So did Pluto.

But the next day
Horace Horsecollar went.
So did Mr. Black.
Mr. Black had seven children.

"There is no room,"
said Mickey.
"There is a lot of room,"
said Mr. Black.

Pluto watched the boat.
He watched and watched.
He did not want to go.

Seven children tried
to play in the boat.
Seven children hopped.
Seven children jumped.

The boat turned over.
People came to help.
"You need a bigger boat,"
said a man.

"Yes," said Mr. Black.
"You could get
a very big boat.
Then people would pay
to ride in it."

"What a good idea,"
said Mickey.
Mickey bought
a very big boat.

A lot of people
went out on
Mickey's boat.

A lot of people
worked on the boat, too.

But Pluto stopped
going with Mickey.

One day Mickey saw Goofy.
Goofy was in his little boat.
Mickey saw Pluto.
Pluto was in
the little boat, too.

Mickey watched the little boat.
He watched and watched.
He wanted to fish.
He wanted to be with Pluto.

The next day Mickey sold
his very big boat.
He bought a small boat.

Mickey and Pluto went fishing.
Mickey did not catch any fish.
He did not care.
He had his boat.
He had his dog.
What more did he need?